THE BEST BIRTHDAY EVER

By Rico Green
Illustrated by the Disney Storybook Art Team

A GOLDEN BOOK • NEW YORK

randomhousekids.com
ISBN 978-0-7364-3619-9 (trade) — ISBN 978-0-7364-3620-5 (ebook)
Printed in the United States of America
10 9 8 7 6

It's Anna's birthday!

Elsa asked Kristoff, Sven, and Olaf to arrive extra early to help decorate the castle courtyard. She wanted everything to be just right for her sister's big day.

Elsa tiptoed into Anna's room. "PSSST. Anna," she whispered.

Anna yawned. "Yeah?" she said, her eyes still closed.

"It's your birthday," said Elsa.

Anna sat straight up. "It's my birthday!" she shouted.

Anna hopped out of bed and changed into
a new birthday dress, made extra special with
Elsa's magic touch.

As Elsa was adding some magical flowers to her own dress, she sneezed. Two tiny snowmen appeared. The snowgies fell to the floor and scampered away before Elsa noticed them.

It was time for presents!
"Just follow the string," Elsa said,
handing one end to Anna.

Anna eagerly followed the string down the hall
and under some furniture . . .

. . . until she ended up at a suit of armor.
There she found a beautiful bracelet!

The string then led to a cuckoo clock with a tiny
Olaf statue that popped out and shouted, "SUMMER!"

Elsa sneezed again, and more snowgies appeared.
But still, no one noticed them.

Next Anna discovered a giant sandwich, and then a new family portrait.

Finding the gifts was a lot of fun, but Elsa's cold was getting worse. More and more snowgies continued to appear—unnoticed—with each sneeze!

A group of snowgies headed for the courtyard. Kristoff and Sven stared at the tiny snowmen in disbelief as they toppled the punch bowl. Elsa was not going to like this!

More snowgies showed up. They launched themselves at the birthday cake! Kristoff grabbed a punch bowl and protected the cake. PHEW! But what mischief would the snowgies get into next?

Meanwhile, as Anna was being led around the kingdom to find even more presents, Elsa was starting to feel feverish.

"This day has been amazing," Anna told her sister. "But I think you need to go home and rest."

"I'm sorry, Anna," Elsa said sadly. "I just wanted to give you one perfect birthday."

"Everything has been wonderful," Anna told her as she pushed open the doors to the courtyard.

"Surprise!" yelled Kristoff and Olaf.

Anna's eyes lit up at the sight of the decorations and her friends—and the huge pile of snowgies! "WOW!"

After everybody sang "Happy Birthday" and enjoyed the cake, Elsa had one more thing to do before heading to bed: blow the royal birthday horn. But as the queen blew, she accidentally sneezed, which sent a giant snowball flying . . .

. . . across the ocean—and right into Hans!

It was finally time for Elsa to rest. Anna got her sister in bed and fed her some warm soup. "BEST BIRTHDAY PRESENT EVER," said Anna.

"Which one?" asked Elsa.

"You letting me take care of you," said Anna.

The sisters smiled at each other. It truly was Anna's best birthday—and it was all thanks to Elsa and their friends.

Not long after the party, there was a knock at the
door of the ice palace. Marshmallow, the giant snowman,
opened the doors. Olaf ran in, surrounded by the little
snowgies.

Kristoff looked at Marshmallow and shook his head.
"Don't ask," he said.